Martha Perry Lowe

The Olive and the Pine

Martha Perry Lowe

The Olive and the Pine

ISBN/EAN: 9783744651820

Printed in Europe, USA, Canada, Australia, Japan

Cover: Foto ©Andreas Hilbeck / pixelio.de

More available books at **www.hansebooks.com**

THE OLIVE AND THE PINE

BY

MARTHA PERRY LOWE

AUTHOR OF "LOVE IN SPAIN," "CHIEF JOSEPH," "BESSIE GREY," ETC.

" Two lands before them passed
In strange and faire contrast "

Second Edition

BOSTON
D. LOTHROP COMPANY
1893

CONTENTS.

PART I. — SPAIN.

Part I.

· S P A I N.

Introduction.

TO THE OLD CASTILIAN KNIGHT.

HAUGHTY soul of bravest story,
Gallant heart of olden glory,
Loyal breast through ages hoary,
      Scorn thou not
      What I have brought.

If I rashly dare to trace
Scenes thy footsteps once did grace, —
I, an alien to thy race, —
      Pardon my
      Temerity.

Touch my verses with the fire
Burning in thee, so my lyre
May some listening hearts inspire
      Unto thy
      Old chivalry.

Scatter down upon my way
The aroma fine which lay
Round thee from the earliest day, —
    Richest bloom
    Of rare perfume!

Thy untaught simplicity,
Studying the fair and high
With no braggart, carping eye,
    Ever be
    Bequeathed to me! —

With the earnestness that brought
Sanctity to every thought,
From the Heavenly Lady caught,
    Shedding bright
    Celestial light; —

And the reverence which o'er
All the world did kneel, adore;
Worshipping in awe before
    God above,
    The highest love.

JOURNEY IN A SPANISH DILIGENCE.

WE journeyed on, o'er hill and plain,
From night till morn, from morn till night :
Ah! who could sleep?   Before the sight
She brought such pictures, — strange old Spain!

The olives, dark and lonely, stand
In dots of verdure o'er the land,
And watch the weary sentinel
Apace the melancholy road,
Who scorns yon lowering cave, — abode
Most dear to robbers' heart, they tell :
The mule-bells jingle on the air,
Impatient of the stillness there.

The master sleeps, — or else is singing
A song which sounds like love, I say,
Did it not grow at once so gay ;
With reckless daring now 'tis ringing!

And all night long he singeth so ;
I strive to catch the note, — but no:
From thoughtless Spain it should not go ;
For us it is too idly sad,
For us it is too wildly glad !

The morning dawns in mountains chill :
I ne'er again my breath shall draw
'Mid such deep loneliness and awe, —
The awe of ages on the spot !
No calm that doth *our* forests fill,
All hushed in work ! — it is the thought
Of what *has been* that makes them still !

The stern old fortress peereth down
For ambushed foe ; she hath forgot
How well she did her work, I wot.
There is no Moor to see her frown !
But old age peaceful cannot now
Smooth out the wrinkles on her brow.

The mellow sun is sinking low :
This hour the good earth tenderer seems,
And full of poesy to grow,
While we are softening into dreams.

We ride up to a wallèd town
Upon a rock, and pass through gates
All hoar with time; yet in them waits
No seer in wisdom's grave renown:
The young sit all day round the walk
Of orange-trees, and idly talk.

We enter fair Sevilla, dimmed
In blinding showers; yet, on the morrow,
We know the rain but mocked at sorrow:
We know she sits, with flowers betrimmed,
Amid her light guitars for aye,
In gay and glad festivity.

A SONG OF THE SUN.

SEVILLE.

THE Sun, how it gloweth, all day gloweth down,
On the gray of thy turrets, O wonderful town!
Sweet Seville, thou'rt riper and fairer to see,
As the ages do touch but to beautify thee:
Sitting there in the sunlight, for centuries dreaming,
How mellow thou growest, as on thee 'tis beaming!

It shines in the face of the beggar who lies
Upturning his brow to the bountiful skies;
And darker and darker and richer it grows,
His locks clinging round it in matted repose:
What cares he, as by him the grander world goes?
Far harder than he they are working, he knows.

Ah, no! 'tis not working that maketh him brown:
The Sun! 'tis the Sun looking steadfastly down!
It feedeth the Spaniard in soul and in sense;
Yes, he'll not be drudging to lay up his pence.
Let him lie in his ragged magnificence,
Till, spell-bound, the artist shall bring him from thence!

The Sun looketh in on the dark myrtle-bowers
Of courts that are sweet with the white orange-flowers,
And golden doth lie on her deep-tinted cheek
Who there at the bars with her lover doth speak.
The bars shut him from her; but he can look through
As well as the Sun, and can touch her cheek too.

Her soft eyes are glowing as evening in June;
And his — they are burning like tropical noon:
'Tis the Sun that is setting on fire the heart!
What cooleth where enters his swift-glowing dart?
Go, rein in his coursers, if here thou wouldst school
The Child of the South by the Northerner's rule!

Now see the rays dance on the gay Guadalquivir!
Along the far plain she's a lonely, sad river,
Where shadows of memory brood over her waves,
As, weary, the desolate Vega she laves;
But here, in dear Seville, she learns to forget,
And smileth in all her young radiance yet!

For all the long day, amid jasmine and roses
And gay promenades, she in beauty reposes;
While fast crowds are floating as butterflies bright,
Or watching the play of the ripples and light,
And orange-groves follow her far on her way
Adown to the sea and to fair Cadiz Bay.

Then streams it aslant the Giralda, the tower
Of the sorrowful Moor, at the soft vesper hour.
Look! fairest old traceries start to the light:
The loiterer standeth amazed at the sight!
So Poesy's glance ever bringeth out plain
The Past's finer etchings to daylight again.

Behold, how it dareth to enter the vast,
The sacred, the holy Cathedral at last!
All mellow, subdued in the window, it lies
Insnared in the maze of those wonderful dyes,
Subliming the colors until they arise,
And float like the souls whom the Lord glorifies.

The Sun, how it gloweth, all day gloweth down,
On the gray of thy turrets, O wonderful town!
Sweet Seville, thou'rt riper and fairer to see,
As the ages do touch but to beautify thee:
Sitting there in the sunlight, for centuries dreaming,
How mellow thou growest, as on thee 'tis beaming!

THE ESCORIAL.

I LOVE the solemn awe that broods around
This spot, so wondrous in its solitude:
'Tis grave, e'en as the ancient faith that walked
In high austerity throughout the land;
'Tis still, as if the many hundred monks
Who lie beneath my feet had e'en but now
To Mary said their prayer, and, one by one,
Crept down below unto their rest in death;
'Tis cold and calm as was the iron front
Of him, its king, who built him here a house,
Where, with his bosom-friend Remorse, he came,
And, in her dread companionship, grew pale
With looking on the blackness of his soul,
And pondering how best to meet his God;
'Tis awful, with its royal dead, who lie
In chill magnificence.
     The mountains gray,
Wherein the Escorial sits, breathe o'er her like
Ascetics rude. The very hedgerows dare

Not seek in graceful longing the glad sky ;
But their young shoots are disciplined unto
A goodly sanctity.

But, ah ! behold
The pages of the ancient manuscripts,
With History's morning twilight, gold and red !
We of the more advancing day have paled
The horizon of our books, as of our lives ;
And in the broad, clear beams of Learning's sun,
We know not the old age's intensity.
The streaks of opening glory then burned in
A deeper coloring to all her thought.

Poor Philip ! I can see thee now, within
The narrow room near by the chapel, where,
'Midst all thy mortal pains, thy gaze was fixed
Upon the altar, while thy dying bed
Was quivering in the mighty organ's roll.
Thy worship's pageantry moved daily o'er
Thy glazing eye : like him who walks the night
In dreams, thou seeing wert, and seeing not.
Ah ! better he, the pure in heart, who makes
His bed beneath the open dome of stars,
And seeth God, the great High Priest, perform
The ritual of the world, and, on the voice
Of answering Nature, passeth unto heaven !

THE VIRGIN OF MURILLO.

MADRID.

BEHOLD her floating radiant on the air!
The laughing cherubs in her lustre play,
Fanned by the waving of her golden hair,
And mantle blue, the robe of purity.
She wears a look of holy, sweet surprise,
Remembering all the words the angel said;
She thinketh of her Son with smiling eyes,
Nor dreameth of that coming hour so dread!—
So fair, celestial in her innocence!
And yet she stood on earth beneath the Tree,
And saw Him lifted up, until from thence
Dear John, belovèd, bore her reverently,
Calming her tears away upon his breast,
And bade her in his home for ever rest.

THE TWO PICTURES.

THE WESTERN HUNTER, AND THE SPANISH MONK.

I.

THERE are two pictures on my wall;
And, when on them my eye doth fall,
I marvel that they side by side
Should be, and yet apart so wide.

One imageth that wild young land
Where roams the grim beast with his band,
And shakes the forests with his cry
Of most exultant liberty; —

The endless waste of waters, where
The lone bird screecheth through the air
In Nature's ear, who sits all day,
And lets her children have their way.

For she, amidst the din, can hear
The distant, tramping feet draw near
Of generations who will crush
Them down, and all their gambols hush; —

E'en as the mother calm doth smile
On her wild brood, and muse the while
How sure thick-coming cares will quell
Ere long the o'er-leaping heart too well.

A rider bursts upon this rude,
Untutored realm of solitude,
And bids his steed with boldness break
His way through yonder treacherous lake.

It is the fierce-eyed Western rover,
With gun and horse for friend and lover :
Ah! little dreams he his last bed
Is making 'neath that horse's tread!

His horse looks in the quiet stream ;
He's looking in red eyes that gleam :
His horse feels but the cooling rushes ;
He feels the hot blood come in flushes.

Defiant, turning, — look at him ! —
He sits, and glares upon a grim
And hungry beast. He stills his breath ;
Is all alive to keep off death !

Methinks I see the monster spring
Upon him as he sits a king,
And pull him from his breathing throne,
Where, Centaur-like, he moved alone, —

And proud surveyed the wilderness, —
Pull him beneath the deep abyss
Of waters; grappling, hide him there,
'Mid weeds and tangles in his hair!

II.

I leave the panting Present now
With noonday sweat upon her brow:
The Past doth steal, with hazy eye,
Like twilight, on my company.

In ancient Spain, where oft amid
The tombs sweet-faced Religion hid, —
Though radiant angels found her out
E'en there, and came and hung about, —

Yon cell beholds a monk in prayer,
While heavenly eyes are watching there:
His locks as streaks of light are flowing,
A silver halo o'er him throwing, —

Caught from the blest, whose faces shine,
So saith the Lord, with looks divine;
And light their Father's kingdom bright,
E'en as the sun, and know not night.

Ah! he is not afraid of Death!
" Come near, that I may feel," he saith,
" How gaunt thou art." Yes, let Death shake
His loosening bones: he will not quake.

He is with him so well acquaint,
That when, at length, the gentle saint
Feels that cold hand upon his brow,
And hears him whisper, " Thy turn now!" —

" Friend, I've been looking out for thee,"
He'll say; then take up quietly
His little cross, and rise and go
With him so meekly, that I know,

Grim Death will stagger back, and stare
On him amazed: " Ah! few do dare
To call me friend: thou robbest me,
Old man! of all my cruelty."

2

Now in those bony arms he'll rest
As sweet as on his mother's breast;
While lights play beauteous o'er his eyes,
Flickering from opening Paradise.

THE MOORISH WELL.

———

How cold, how crisping, and how sweet!
The traveller climbs, with languid feet,
The fair Alhambra crownèd hill:
The eager water, calm and still,
In crystal quiet deftly lies
To charm him with a quick surprise.

He comes, — he grasps in ardent haste
The draught, and long and deep doth taste:
It startles him with joyance clear,
Like silver bells a-sounding near;
So keen, so laughter-like, so springing,
Through all his being it is ringing.

It cutteth swift through every vein,
Like sudden castanets again,
Which in and out do run and patter
About the ear with gentle clatter:
His soul is dancing down and up
Unto the music of the cup.

But list! a showery vision light
Sparkles in grace before his sight:
A dark-browed Moorish creature there!
The fountains tangle in her hair;
From out her eyes in jets they ray,
In curves around her mouth they play.

"O Christian! know that thou dost sip
From out the well that cooled my lip,
When, in a raging, burning thirst,
A faithless Spanish knight I cursed; —
Ay, cursed the Holy Virgin even,
By whom he swore to me and Heaven!

"He of the Cross, in stern amaze,
Came down before my trembling gaze:
'Blasphemest thou the Mother, — she
Who stood by me on Calvary?
For this shalt thou insnarèd lie
Below to all eternity!'"

She sank beneath the earth in spray,
Doomèd to linger there for aye,
And pour her life out to the fount:
The stranger feels his blood remount,
And well up high with drops that start
Fresh from a Moslem maiden's heart!

CAROLINA CORONADO,

POETESS OF SPAIN.

THE walls of Badajoz looked down
Upon a gifted maid, who rose
Within that old, beleaguered town,
And startled Spain from her repose.

Her eyes were beaming with the fire
Of poet youth beneath her dark
And shining locks.   She struck her lyre;
And, lo! the land of Spain did hark.

She calmed her deep, impassioned breast
With love to all the solitudes,
And hid beside the wild-bird's nest
Her verses in the rocks and woods.

She hung enraptured on the sweet
Young meadow rose, and lingered near
The turtle-dove, who did repeat
" Love, love," for ever in her ear.

Unto the Stars she told her tale,
Weeping her tears melodiously
At evening with the Nightingale,
Or with the Palm communing high.

Her genius moved not straight within
The prunèd walks of classic time,
But ran abroad, and revelled in
New laws that rose from out her rhyme.

She poured a tide of passion through
The sordid flats of Life's dull sea;
And, last, she dared to speak unto
Her nation that word — Liberty!

Yes, she — the fearless girl — did make
The slavish priesthood tremble at
The burning words of truth she spake,
And poets at her footstool sat.

At length the laurel wreath they set
Upon her in the royal dome;
But most she loves the coronet
Of wife and mother in her home!

BOABDIL.

BEHOLD him bowed upon the little hill,
That sits in meekness all the day, forlorn,
Beneath the proud Alhambra's fiery eye,
Who speaketh from her height in palest scorn : —

" Ay, keep him fair-haired, silken hero, made
Of pensive moonbeams and the whispering breeze !
Ay, keep him of the blue eyes, so afraid
To guard my towers, who skulks through yonder trees !

" Receive his sighs upon your nursing breast, —
'Tis softer than my bosom, sweeter bed : —
He loves the cooling grass, the wooing rest,
More than the flashing fire around my head.

---

* " Last Sigh of the Moor," the name of the little hill where
Boabdil retired, and mourned for the Alhambra.

" Ah ! sing a song of love to make him sleep
    Among your coverts, so he may not hear
    The booming thunder — bid him not to weep —
    'Tis sweeter than his sighing to my ear!

" And let your gentlest airs a languid haze
    Breathe o'er him, that he may not see the smoke
    That gathers round my throat, nor mark the blaze
    That flashes on my face as lightning stroke.

" Hark ! hear I not, 'mid clanging hosts that move,
    My King, who bids me, as some lady's lyre,
    A fond farewell?   Peace ! peace ! no words of love,
    Boabdil, since thou hast no deeds of fire ! "

———

THE KING.

" O thou Alhambra, beautiful and bright,
    Who sat'st serene amid the stars and sun,
    Gazing in high repose, at morn and night,
    O'er all the world, — adieu, thou glorious One!

" O mighty arm, that held in glory through
    The rolling years the heroes safe and well ;
    And breasted back the flaming darts that flew
    Anigh their lofty hearts invincible ; —

"And swept the blackening, deadly hail away,
So it could shatter not one beauteous form;
·And laughed, in exultation proud and gay,
To see their locks untouched amid the storm! —

"Thou paradise, exceeding beautiful,
Wherein the lovely eyes have darkly glanced
Among the rapturous fountains sleeping cool,
That sprang to hear their footsteps light, and
danced! —   ,

"No more the maids shall lie within thy doors,
Beneath the whiteness of thy silvery walls,
While their black tresses sweep along the floors
'Mid gold and blue that gleam from Afric's halls!

"I will not stay with thee! — by Allah, no!
Since I an arm of help no more can reach:
I will not see thee 'midst a glaring foe,
Nor hear the pompous Christian's rolling speech!

"Alhambra! glory of my soul! my love!
Forget not him who turns away his face:
He, for thy sake, with bleeding heart must rove
Without a land, — a home, — a resting-place!

" Farewell! and guard thou sweet Granada, while,
The Crescent sinking pale upon her crest,
Thy King hath ceased in dreams of thee to smile,
And laid him down to deep, unbroken rest!"

She trembled when she heard his words, — the great,
Fair Lady, — watching him afar with sighs
And looks of love, until the film that sate
Around her forehead dimmed her eagle eyes.

And then she roused herself again to meet
The grappling of the Spanish men: they prest
On her for Christ and victory, sure and sweet: —
At morn the eternal Cross was on her breast!

WHAT THE ANDALUSIAN GUITAR SAYS.

RING, ring, ring, ring,
Merry, merry Castanet!
Sing, sing, sing, sing,
Maiden, with your eyes of jet!

Clickety clack, clickety clack,
Anda, anda! forward and back!
Hear me humming, humming, humming!
Hear me tumming, tumming, tumming!

Life — it is precious and fair and sweet;
Death — it is dark, and the grave ye meet:
Gather the moments! — quick! they are flying;
Gather the sunbeams! — see! they are dying.

Fading, fading, fading away, —
Tum-a-lum, lum,
Ting-a-ling, ling:
Faster, faster, faster, I play;
Whirling and twirling, I'll keep ye for aye!

The priest — let him stare;
And what do ye care?
I'll buzz in his ear
A tune he shall hear,
That will drown all his aves and long pater-noster,
And worry the old monk who sits in his cloister.

But, ah! in my song,
If you list to it long,
There are strains that do rove
Through the shadows of love,
With sobbing pulsation
And throbbing vibration,
That wake in the spirit a swift perturbation.

How silver the moonlight, how gracious the breeze,
Looking into the lattice, at play in the trees!
Ah! love is the radiant charmer of night,
That whispers untroubled the hopes of the light,
And lingers in full-breathing ecstasy sweet,
Or parts all tumultuous, never to meet!

O sorrowful, sorrowful children of earth!
I weep for ye wildly, — weep over your birth;
I sigh out the pains that are rending your breast;
I sing of the hearts that have entered their rest,
Divided no more in the land of the blest!

But hush, my complain,
Begone with this strain!
Dear Love! he is weeping;
The moonbeams are creeping,
And mournfulest cadence your footsteps are keeping.
Up, up! the Bolero moves tardily on:
Away with the breaking of hearts that are gone!
Fly on to the maze of advance and retreat,
And slide through the air with your rapturous feet!

THE BULL-FIGHT.

SEE wave on wave arise
Of swaying human heads,
And flashing, coal-black eyes,
And fluttering fan that spreads
Around the costly scent
From glossy, woven braids,
With gold and crimson blent
Of thousand Spanish maids!

The Infanta towereth high,
In gleam of jewels hid!
Of fair nobility
She crowns the pyramid.
The princely children sit
Around with chattering glee:
Their cheeks blench not a whit
At thought of what's to be!

But, hark! the trumpets sound;
The Bull is in the ring;
The goaders stand around, —
The red, red cloth they fling:
It blazes on his brain!
He runneth wild about,
To tear the thing in twain.
Come, Picador! — come out!

The Bull drives on in wrath,
When, lo! a sudden thrust
Doth send a crimson path
Streaking along the dust!
Now springs he on the foe:
A dainty man is he,
With airy dress, and show
Of gentler revelry.

His horse doth shake in all
His sinews mightily.
Not so the rider small;
With calm and glittering eye,
He meets that plunging head
That sets itself for fight,
With shock of lance so dread,
It swoons in dizzy sight.

The monster sickens fast;   .
He will not rouse again:
Yes, yes! the swoon is past!
He rallies from his pain;
He gives a sidelong sweep,
And whelms the horse in death, —
Lashing, as doth the deep
The drowning sailor's breath.

.

The Picador is down
As lightning from his seat,
And leaves the Bull alone,
The dead horse at his feet.
Look, look! — the Matador!
He kneels before the court,
And humbly craveth for
Their grace to end the sport.

The royal will he learns, —
A gracious boon it is;
And gratefully he turns
To meet the Bull, I wis!
O Matador! thou must
Put up thy sword from sight,
Nor give a single thrust,
Till he begins the fight.

What stillness now doth reign
O'er all the gazing mass!
Before his crowded brain
A thousand ages pass!
Eternally he lies
Beneath that goring head;
Eternally he dies,
With sudden tossings dread!

One second stands he still;
One leap the great Bull makes:
Then with such steady will
His mortal aim he takes,
The weapon darteth straight
Betwixt the neck and breast,
And sitteth there in state,
In sheath of purple drest!

With what a mighty fall
The monster sinks to earth!
" Bravo!" the myriads call,
With trumpets' clanging mirth.
The mules, bespangled bright,
Trot in the arena's bound,
And drag him out of sight,
Low on the abasèd ground.

Go, fair Infanta, dream
Of bloody death to-day!
Thy little children seem
To see it when they pray.
And, lo! the nations far
Do point, with warning hand,
To yonder stains that are
Upon thy native land!

.

MALAGA, — THE REST.

MALAGA, thou noiseless haven sweet,
Offering thy blessed, kind retreat
Gently to the weary, languid feet! —

How thou drawest thy blue curtain there,
Shutting from the wildered eye the glare,
And the cold and chilling northern air!

Golden is the lamp which thou dost trim:
Never for the sufferer is it dim;
Shedding mellow, pensive light on him.

Beautiful, caressing, airy room!
Castles on thy sky for pictures loom,
Cheering oft his spirit's sickly gloom;

Stretching out, as flowing tapestry,
Yonder rainbow-tinted, velvet sea,
Folding round his footsteps coolingly!

Hush! how still the air around his rest,
Smoothing down the ripples in his breast,
Where the swift disturber, Pain, hath prest!

They are waiting in thy beauteous hall,
When the flowers open, — when they fall;
Waiting for one lovely presence, all.

And perchance she comes with dimpled cheek,
Roses blushing soft when she doth speak,
Bounding rapturous to the sufferer meek.

Ah! she oftener steals anear with eye
Pitiful; then turns her silently,
Shakes her head, and says a kind good-by.

HUSBAND AND WIFE.

FROM ENGLAND TO MALAGA.

THEY sat together there so still, —
She, calm and holy, moist-eyed dove;
He, keen and restless, strong of will,
Made soft and tender now by love:
Her being strengthened in its beams;
His melted in o'erflowing streams.

He came from far, with heart o'erleaping, —
The miles so long, the hours so creeping, —
Oft chafing to himself; but then
A thought came to him suddenly:
" God ! " said he, " should I never see
Her large eyes look in mine again,
Nor feel her fingers laid on me,
How restful were this weariness !
How sweet such idle pain as this ! "

But she *did* smile again on him.
He thought upon that vision grim
That broke so sharp on his complaining,
So quick his fretful tongue restraining;
And laughed to see the phantom dim
Before her lustrous gaze was waning:
" 'Twas false!" he cried defiantly.
But, when he saw her earnest eye,
He seized the folding of her gown,
And kissed it while the tears fell down.
She did not ask him why he took
Her dress so wild, — what made him look
Again so humble and so meek.
She knew: then wherefore bid him speak?
Watch o'er his soul she oft had kept,
And laid its strangest workings by,
Within her dear, fond memory;
But most the changing clouds that swept
O'er his fair heaven of love; and, though
They marred its deep sereneness so,
She thought they did but touch it new
With varying and changing hue,
Leaving a deeper, brighter glow.

Fond, blessed hearts, that stirred by turns,
And calmed each other's bosoms so,

Cooling the daily fever-burns, —
Why should they not together go
Upon the lone and darksome sea
That stretches to Eternity?
His tender, fragile bird — could he
Bear see her spread herself alone?
Her wild and fevered mate — would she
Leave him to flutter here, and moan?
Could she contented rest her wings
Beneath the Tree of Life on high,
When on his prison-bar he springs,
And falls down chill, despairingly?

The Sabbath sun was sinking low, —
And she arose, and touched some chords
Of music sweet, and sang these words:
" The Lord my Shepherd is; and, though
Along the vale of death I go,
I will not shrink, nor be afraid
To meet alone the dreadful shade!"

Then went she back unto him there.
His head upon his hands did rest:
She laid them softly on her hair,
As if she came to be caressed.
And, as they sat so still and dreamed,
An angel took the harp, it seemed,

And sang: " Ah, children, who abide
On mortal earth, and love and fear!
Rest ye in peace.   God will provide
A way to part ye gently here.
If love's dear flame doth temper right
Your souls, and burn them pure and white,
So kind he'll still the precious breath,
Ye'll stand in wondering peace by Death."

JEALOUS.

———

Dolores! dost thou love him? — say!
No! silence, girl! for thee I hate!
I saw him look at thee to-day:
Was it for that he came so late?

I saw thee moving on the walk,
Nor ever stirred thy treacherous eye:
How sweetly he with me did talk!
Yet felt he not thy passing-by?

A curse be on thy ankles light,
To trip thee in thy fair design!
A thousand plagues descend, and write
Their mark upon that cheek of thine!

He said that I was handsome too!
He said my eyes were wondrous bright;
That he could see them flashing through
The very deepest, deepest night!

They'll flash throughout this night of pain,
I tell thee, girl! if this be so;
And cut thy purposes in twain,
And *burn* thee, ere from life I go!

But thou art soft and sweet and still;
Dost lure him with a single thought:
He will obey thy secret will,
And think that thou commandest not.

Thy pretty hands are small and white:
A dagger did they ever hold?
It looketh clear and smooth and bright;
But, ah! it feels so very cold!

Thou wilt be colder yet to see
How warm the place to which it darts;
Paler, to look at him and me,
With blood avenging both our hearts!

FORSAKEN.

DOLORES! dost thou weep?
   Speak it again to me!
Or did I dream in sleep,
   That what I said to thee
Thou sworest to forget?
   For Jesu's blessed sake,
   Thou wilt the promise make!
Ah, yes! thine eyes are wet!

   And I was dreaming, child;
So hard thou wouldst not be!
   The vision 's made me wild;
But now my soul is free.
   Blood, blood, was on my heart!
I dreamed! — but God was kind:
He held me, mad and blind!

   Speak, speak, ere I depart!
Is it not true, to-night
   Lorenzo's pulses beat? —
He sees the blessed light,
   The grass beneath his feet?

I loved him, — oh, 'twas bliss!
No more, no more, of this!
Away! — I enter where
No passion stains the air!
Love! cruel was thy blow;
　　But now the weight of sin
From off my soul doth go;
　　My breast is calm within.
Sweet Virgin Mother! hold
　　The hearts of lovers here:
When they are growing cold,
　　Blest Mother! be thou near,
And still the raging tide
Of burning grief and pride!
Jesu! my pain, my sin,
　　Take all upon thy cross.
　　The world to me is dross:
Oh! let me enter in,
　　And hide beneath thy name
　　My poverty and shame!
Sweet Mother! — Death is here!
Where am I? — Come! — I fear! —
Wipe off this heavy sweat, and stay,
And lead me; for 'tis dark upon the way.

ALDONZA, THE YOUNG SINGER.

SHE sat beneath the swaying Palm
That whispered Eastern memories;
While, in its every wave, the balm
Of old perfumèd lays did rise.
She walked at early morning light,
And toned the glistening lyre of youth;
Then sat serene at pensive night,
And sang her songs of love and truth.

She saw the shepherd moving by,
And followed him, the lambs among:
He went his way all silently,
Nor wondered at her prattling tongue;
While she took up each tender thing,
And held it on her sheltering arm,
Or fondest praises oft would sing —
And press it to her bosom warm —
Of the sweet Lamb of Innocence,
Within the church not far from thence,

Who sitteth on his Mother's knee
To light the altar wondrously.

The little red moon, hiding by
Nevada's steep, she questioned free
And fearlessly, and wondered why
'Twas blushing deep and angry then;
And why so calm and pale again
Through all the night, as though a thought
Of restless passion touched it not.

To gather flowers she would stop, —
The scarlet corn-flower and the bright
Fair gold and purple asters drop
Within her lap, and amaranths white.
She thought them robed in Paradise,
And deemed they left with their wet eyes
The radiant, flowery band so sweet,
Who round the Virgin's skirts do cling,
And lay themselves around her feet,
Again with freshening looks to fall
Beneath her step ethereal.

She was a woman: they drew nigh
To mark her deep, poetic eye,
Her beauty and benignity,

Where'er her gentle footsteps moved;
And, ah! she loved,—and, ah! she loved,—
And felt the sweet and bitter fears
That come with love, and wept the tears
And heard the beating never cease
Of doubt and hope and pain and peace,
And last despair,—the bitterest;
For he was false unto her heart.
He struck a pain unto the breast
Which he had sheltered and caressed;
He sent a quick and sudden smart
Upon a gentle soul's delight,—
Then fled for ever from her sight!

She was a woman,—ay, indeed!
And she was ready, at his need,
To lay aside her fancy's wings,
Her lovely, fair imaginings,
Forget her songs, and slight the powers
Which used to fire her radiant hours;
Accepting but the joy to bring
To him her faithful ministering,
And walk the simple way of earth,
Like those of poor and lowliest worth,
And love and serve,—the highest heaven
And humblest to a woman given!

She would have laid beneath his feet
Her lyre, with but a lullaby
For ever sounding clear and sweet
A low, deep song of constancy ! —
No! he was faithless, that alone
The world might have her for its own.

Where was she now, bewildered one?
Gone was her singing heart, and gone
Her heart of love. The singing she
Had cast aside for loving: he,
The lover, had despoiled her breast
First of its young, poetic rest,
Then of its sweet disquietude;
And left a weary, empty pain
To fill her spirit's solitude.
The songs — they would not come again,
Nor drown the ceaseless, ceaseless ring
Of Love's still footsteps echoing!
She roamed in pitiful young grief,
Weeping her fond and vain belief;
Then sat in stillest apathy:
And so the changeless days went by.

But once, as she was wandering slow
Betwixt the spirit's storm and lull, —

Her heart not heaving too and fro,
Nor lying tranquilly and full, —
She saw the Virgin, heavenly eyed,
Gathering, in meadows by her side,   ,
The whitest amaranths that e'er
Grew starry on this brown earth drear;
And with the white her golden hair
Gleamed out in blinding radiance there.
Aldonza sank upon her knee,
And bowed her head; but presently
She felt cool hands upon her laid,
Like sacred streams from Olivet,
Laving her quiet locks of jet:
It was — it was the holy Maid!
She knew the amaranth as it wound
About her temples, and around
She felt a glory, — ah! so nigh!
She dared not look; but silently
She prayed: when rose she from the ground,
The radiant lady was not there;
The wreath had melted in her hair.

So she took up her lyre again,
And sang, — ah! how divinely then! —
Until they, one by one, broke forth,
Children of this distracted earth,

From thickening press of cares and sighs,
Or smoother bond of gayeties,
To hear her songs.   The sweetest sadness,
The purest and the soberest gladness,
That ever came from lips so young,
Fell on them as Aldonza sung.

For Love had left its fulness deep,
Nor sorrow's presence dark could sweep
The gracious impress of that tread
Away — Love's footstep vanishèd!
Yet *him* she named not, — breathed not 'mong
Her lays: there silent was her tongue.
He was beloved of her, not sung.
But all the springs, so pure and sweet,
That Love unseals, when souls do meet
It sacredly, bedewed her song.
She sang of truth, nobility;
Of loftiness and courage strong;
Of goodness and of charity;
And of the Cross, — consoler deep, —
With gentlest tears for eyes that weep;
And of our sins and fears, — with grace
Of hope and patience on her face.

The young men bowed, in kindling awe,
Around her; and the maids would draw

Anear, and kiss her robe, the while:
The old would pass her by, and smile,
And say the saints to her had given
Some benediction fresh from heaven.
They gathered up, when by her side,
Her songs, and bore them far and wide
Through all España's restless marts
Of throbbing breasts and fiery hearts.
A spirit beautiful she grew:
Her land was all aglow with her.
In modest lustre, into view
She rose a heavenly messenger, —
A charmèd presence rose, — to meet
Sweet homage laid beneath her feet;
While she, the Spanish girl, among
Her waving palms, unconscious sung.

At length they crowned her with the wreath
That cools the poet's brow beneath;
That overshadoweth, deep and green,
His weary, wandering vision keen;
And calms the fervor of his eye
With dew of immortality.

And once they found her, at the light
Of early summer stars, asleep

In peace among the amaranths white
That circled starry round her breast, —
A silver halo o'er her rest, —
A radiant bed, from which they bore
Her soul to the immortal shore.
The Virgin called, — and she was taken:
She was asleep, — no more to waken!

MARCELA.

Is not she
Brightest gem you e'er did see;
Very best
Jewel on Sevilla's breast?

Happy sprite!
Now she cometh, flashing light,
Airy sparkling,
Out beneath her eyebrows darkling.

Rolleth rich
From her lips the Spanish speech,
Pouring out
Golden streams of talk about.

Rising gay,
Airily she steps away,
Fashioning
Jauntily a look to fling.

" Ah ! you know
I am handsome ; but I go ! "
    Seems to you
This she says with her adieu.

From the next
Parts she just as tender?   Vext
    Are you by
Her benignant coquetry?

Better spite
Southern zephyrs, dancing light !
    They and she
Only live to flutter free.

Better run
From the royal Southern sun !
    Is not he
Ever courting ceaselessly?

You alone
Are the very dullest drone:
    Where doth fly
Your new foreign suavity?

How it clung —
Your poor, niggard Saxon tongue —

In its place,
With no answering back of grace!

Was it not
Your slow-moving, Northern thought
Made you shy
Of her Andalusian eye?

If the sea
Of creation throweth free
Myriad host,
Like you not what sparkles most?

Look again
For another, nor complain:
Nature keeps
Gems for all, among her deeps.

THE MAJO.

PEASANT DANDY.

——

Who is there so gay
As I the livè-long day?
Who can dress so well?
Sir, I pray you, tell.
You are English, friend?
Come, your eye-glass lend, —
Peering up so high
Into Spanish sky.
        Yola, hola, ha!

While I'm seeing clear
All about me here,
You read your red book
Ere you dare to look:
Come along, and be
Happy, sir, like me!
Soft, Amigo, now
I will show you how.
        Yola, hola, ha!

Crimson mantle bright
Round my waistcoat tight;
Buttons jingling neat
Down unto my feet, —
Shaking silvery
When the girls go by;
While they stop and stare,
All in love, I swear!
  Yola, hola, ha!

Broidered jacket close,
Till to me it grows;
And my flat Sombrero, —
Look you, Estrangero,
When you would be free,
Up to any joke,
Own it then to me!
Don my hat and cloak!
  Yola, hola, ha!

I can sing a song,
Till they dance along,
Springing from afar
Round my good guitar.
I can ride a fleet
Pony through the street;

And the girls will sigh,
Oh! so pensively!
    Yola, hola, ha!

I can whisper sly
Through the lattice, — ay!
Rita knoweth best
Who is handsomest!
If she does forget,
There are black eyes yet:
Other maids there be
Who will talk with me.
    Yola, hola, ha!

Kings and queens and priests,
Grandees, eat your feasts!
Only do not veto
My good cigarito!
Sorry English-man,
Learning all you can,
May your worship flee us:
Go you home with Dios!
    Yola, hola, ha!

RIBERA'S PICTURE OF AN OLD MONK.

THOU good old man, what errand wouldst thou do,
When some pale artist, with high ardor full,
Caught thee upon his canvas, clear and true,
In all thy sweetness so ineffable?

Ah! thou art leaning on young Charity;
She guides — that mild, dear saint — from place to place:
So long hast thou been in her company,
That thou hast caught her looks upon thy face.

She cannot smooth the pillow round thy head,
But drops her tears that thou wilt lay thy hairs
So white upon a lean and shrivelled bed,
Through all thy ministry and weary cares.

Yet, if thou bidst her ever lead the way
Through sorrow, self-denial cannot keep
Its watch around thy dreams: will she not stay
To nurse thee *then*, when thou art gone to sleep;

And sing to thee of Him, the Morning Star,
And them whose road through tribulation lay
To where the sounds of many waters are,
And He is wiping all the tears away;

Until a smile goes over thee most sweet,
And runs adown thy beard in silver light;
As if thou, in thy dreams, hadst sprung to meet
The Shepherd with thy crown of glory bright?

THE ORGAN-PLAYER.

He sat there at the great old Organ's side
In mastery complete, and slowly laid
His fingers on the silent keys, and felt
Them o'er with groping hands, as he were rapt
Within the mazes of a wandering dream.

But, lo! the waking!   Suddenly uprose
A mighty tempest of great notes, that rolled
Through all the carvèd space, and shook it from
Its boundless marble plains away unto
The spangled grayness of its lofty dome;
And trembled in the arches, fading off
Till where they caught the rosy bloom that streamed
From little windows set with precious stones,
That looked aslant the vastness, cutting through
With rainbow mists the silent clouds of dark.
He is undaunted 'mid the whirlwind of
High ecstasy and pain, and joy and grief,

Which he hath wakened; for his soul is far
Ascending to the upper dome that rests
Its beams not underneath the stars and sky,
Like this fair atom in the eye of heaven.
He sees his bride, who walketh in the light
That plays immortal in her hazel eyes,
And broods around her hair at rest in folds
Of placid brownness on her mellow cheek.

She is not roving 'mong the glorified,
Forgetful of the restless hearts on earth:
She watches him below with earnest eyes,
And lays her ear unto the floor of heaven
To catch the earthly sounds that wander up.
She follows close upon the Organ's sweep
With voice of sweetness, full and deep and low.
He hears it, — 'mid the cooling shadow of
The great Cathedral, hears it day and night, —
An undertone for ever sounding clear
Throughout the torrent of his whelming chords.
Said he not, 'twas no mortal hands that ruled
The harmonies amid that solitude?
And so he sitteth there at morn and even,
And fondly dreameth that some time he may
Float hence upon the current of her voice
Unto the high concerto of the skies!

VALENCIA.

HOMEWARD WITH E——.

DEAREST companion, Spain has passed from sight:
Dost thou remember that luxurious hour
When we, entranced, were walking 'neath the power
Of evening, music, beauty, love, and light;
The pleasant sadness stealing o'er us so,
As we bethought us how no longer we
Amid the children of the Sun should be,
But soon shut in with thickening winter's snow;
Not where the pulses lie in languid ease,
But where they spring to meet an enemy, —
The sovereign Cold, — and conquer him, or die?
Yet that far land we chose beyond the seas:
One lulled us with a dream of Lotus-trees;
The other woke to fair Reality.

THE STEAM-ENGINE IN MADRID.

STRANGE monster, who hath sent thee dashing thus
Profaningly through these old time-worn shores?
Thy sailing vapors are in fast pursuit,
Though some do tarry oft to wreathe themselves
Amid the listless, waving Spanish air;
Now playful hid, now creeping out again,
Forgetful of their rushing fiery work,
Insnared beneath the dreamy Southern sky.

A goodly sight: yet wherefore do I turn
Mine eyes away from fair Castilla's plains,
The soil of silver speech and gentle blood;
From yon blue mountains rising up so grave,
Like heart of ancient Spanish warrior;
And that fair city gleaming at their feet,
Seat of the proudest line of monarchy?
It is because it minds me of that land,
So young and strong, that stretches out its arms —

Its interlacing arms — o'er all the earth;
And sweeter than its greatness is the thought,
That there I drew the breath of liberty:
For that belovèd, far-off land is home.
O my America! the eyes of all
Now eager wait to see what thou canst do:
Be faithful in thy promise to the world!

5

TO WASHINGTON IRVING.

If there be any who have listened to
My songs, it was because thou wentst before ;
Because thy master-hand a picture drew
Touched with the very look España wore.

And it was painted with a brush so rare,
So smooth, so lightsome, in its workmanship,
That men stood all entranced in pleasure there,
And wondered why the hours so fast did skip.

The colors were in richening soberness
Laid on, with flitting hues of light and shade,
That glow for ever, like the Virgin's dress,
And never from our native sky shall fade.

America stood still amid her chase
Through glaring daylight and reality,
And dreamed with thee among that twilight race,
Until it softened down her fevered eye.

Perchance, if thou shouldst scan these songs of mine,
They'd wake within thee pensive memories,
Or mind thee how that legend-page of thine
Is gilded with thy country's fondest praise.

And if I have no power to charm her, then
Mayhap she will turn back, when I do sing,
From counting o'er her gold, to look again
Upon the costlier treasures thou didst bring.

Part II.

NEW ENGLAND.

THE ROAD OVER THE HILLS.

I love, each lingering summer afternoon,
When stay the hours, so loath to part with June,
Beside my window with a book to sit,
And let my eye from off its pages flit
Away, away, to yonder distant wood,
Where creeps along, in lovely solitude,
The village road; now here, now there, so white,
Climbing the hill-top, cheerily and bright,
Amid the pine-trees hushed and dark as night.

At length, I seem in fancy there to be
Among the young flowers, by the green wayside,
That sit and look so sweet and earnestly
Upon the traveller who doth by them ride.
How still it is! The squirrel quick hath run
Across the track unto the old gray wall
Wreathed o'er with thorny vines, while brambles tall
Beset it round; and 'neath the summer sun

Floats the bronzed butterfly, until — behold ! —
His wings are turning all to burnished gold !
And all day, in the wild young cricket's ear,
The locust proseth ; but she will not hear.
And, hark ! a sudden stream of melody
Comes quivering through the calm and silent wood :
'Tis the sweet thrush, far from the gazing eye,
Who swelleth now her little gushing throat
Alone for her dear mate and tender brood ;
And, ere the air hath caught that lovely note,
'Tis gone, and all the woods are dark and lone :
And long they wait expectant of that tone,
Nor know they where she sits, until again
Her music runneth quick through all their bowers, ·
And ceaseth.   Ah ! no nightingales of Spain,
That sing at night around Grenada's towers,
So fondly all my ear and heart did gain.

I dream the farmer windeth down the hill,
And wonder if this loveliness will fill
His soul, and touch him now one-half so sweet
As me, adown upon the nimble feet
Of Fancy borne, or on the airy wings
Of swift Imagination, light and free ;
Or thinks he only of the corn that springs ·
And groweth now so bravely, but to be

Ere long within his petty barn, to feed
Him and his little ones in time of need?
Ah! he is poor, and they must eat and drink:
He has no time on such as ye to think,
Sweet images of God's great beauteousness!
But ye forget not him, nor serve him less:
Your gentle influence will enter deep
Beyond the sunburn, and the callousness
Of pinching wintry frosts, and still doth keep
Until he sitteth with his little girl,
And playeth with some golden dropping curl,
At evening-hour, beneath the cottage-door.
Then ye do make him wander back once more
To his forgotten youth and days gone by;
And, while he looks upon his little child,
He'll wipe a tear perchance from out his eye.
He sees again his mother's blue eyes mild
Smiling her boy to school each opening day;
And him, the generous friend, the spirit wild,
Who thought no more of death than he at play,
And yet so early left him on the way, —
So early laid him down to earth, and slept!
And then he thinks how he is longer kept
In this hard-working world, and draweth deep
A sigh that he might ere long fall to sleep.

Meanwhile comes forth the early star of even,
Or else the goldèn harvest moon doth rise,
The festive Autumn emblemed in the heaven!
And he will rest his soul, and lift his eyes
Unto the Harvest Home in yonder skies!

THE OCEAN AT BEVERLY.

I AM afraid of thee, old Ocean! thou
Dost fill me with unutterable awe.
The gentle maiden calls thee beautiful;
The youth doth love thee, — thou so gallant, brave;
The hero stern, because thou art defiant,
Unyielding as his own relentless breast;
And, last, the poet loveth thee, who art
As boundless as the vague, eternal longings
That sweep across his soul, — now gently swayed,
Now swelling all his being mightily!
But, when I gaze upon thee, I do think
That there is nought but thee and me alone, —
No life, nor joy nor hope; nor ever was,
Nor ever will be, any thing save thee,
Stretching for ever on a mighty waste, —
One great eternity of desolation!

THE PICNIC.

Sweet golden hours, intense with early joy and pain!
I dream of them in smiles that come and go in tears, —
In tears of tenderness for all the vanished years,
In smiles of peace that asks their presence not again.

The west wind freshens round Monadnock pale,
And shakes away his vaporous cap of night,
Until he wakes majestic to invite
The children of the Ashuelot Vale.

There is a wondrous meaning in his gaze:
" O village men and maidens! hear the voice
Of Nature when her spirit doth rejoice!
I sit alone, and list to all she says.

" I hear her sweet, low song at early light;
Or, while she sleeps at noon with glowing cheeks,
I mark her breathing, till she murmuring speaks,
And wakes, at hush of eve, serene and bright.

" Come ! come, and be of her sweet life a part:
Away, poor Care ! and hide thy palsied head;
And, stately Sorrow ! raise thee from thy dead,
To rest upon thy living mother's heart."

They hear his speech, — the mountain grand !
It runs electric, hand to hand;
And in and out, with busy feet,
They throng the peaceful village street.
They come from pleasant doors in green
Of darksome Maple shut from day;
Or where the slender Elms are seen
In swinging high-born grace at play;
Or out of cool piazzas, light
With sun, and dark with clinging vine
Of grape, whose spraying shadows twine
Along the steps to line their feet;
Or down the slopes of grass so bright,
And glistening with the dewdrops sweet.

The little lad, with eager eye,
Is running, high his basket swinging,
And braves the children going by
With laugh to hear the dull bell ringing.

The blue-eyed maid who slowly passed
But yesterday with book o'erbent,

Her guileless soul too soon harássed
By learning's dim bewilderment;
Her brow, too full of growing thought,
To-day is wearing once again
The roses which her girlhood brought,
Where late the fragile lilies stood
Of eager-dawning womanhood.

The graceful matron of the home,
Who keeps the springs of its dear life
In order 'mid the jar and strife, —
Serene and watchful, she will come.

And they, the grave-browed men, who've seen
The generations step between
Them and the forms they loved to meet, —
'Tis but a day since, — in the street,
Forget the sleeping ones to-day,
And join the smiling band, awake
To joy and hope and liberty,
To glory, love, and life, awake!

The fleecy clouds are floating in the blue,
The green of summer deepens ever new,
Till full refreshment sinks upon the sated view.

They move along in calm repose of noon,
And drink the beauty of the glowing June:
All care shall lie down calmly at her young feet soon.

The mountain, wrapt in purple noontide haze,
In veilèd beauty slumbers on their gaze,
And floats away as they approach in soft amaze.

His slumberous calm is creeping slowly nigh
To fold them in the sweet tranquillity
Of souls, with all the universe in tune for aye.

Arouse! the Lake! yon sparkling drop
Down in the mountain's pebbly cup,
That looks from fringèd eyelid up,
And, smiling, dreams that she has pressed
The strong Monadnock to her breast,
Ethereal in her liquid rest;
Nor vexes her sweet thoughts as we,
Who oft so vainly disagree
'Twixt shade and substance foolishly.
— So, with the Lake the journey done,
They fall entrancèd, one by one,
Into the rocky nooks at ease,
Or lean against the o'erhanging trees
To watch this jewel in the sun.

The shining stone, that once did rest
'Neath her caresses, now again
Goes skimming back upon her breast,
From lady's hand that quivers still,
Or firm and manly arm that fain
Would not outvie the maiden's skill,
Yet aims it with a steadier will.

Ere long the baskets open wide,
And all survey them satisfied:
The napkins glisten on the grass
In lavish generosity,
Piled up with bounties rich that pass
Around by maidens trippingly:
Nor she of most ethereal mind,
Nor he by city thin refined,
Of being exquisite and rare,
Could here withstand the buxom air,
Or stay the human needs that in
Untrammelled spirits joy within
The freedom of simplicity.

They help the tirèd children first,
Their little tongues are so athirst;
For here there is no stately rule:
Dame Nature keeps to-day the school.

Will she not shock the old *régime*
That kept the elders in their seat,
While children's waiting eyes did gleam
With hungry looks to see them eat?

The shades of afternoon are coming on;
The fitful gleaming of the Lake is gone:
It lies subdued within the mellow light,
And wins serener homage at the night.

The little boat creeps outward from the shore,
And handsome cheeks are browning at the oar;
While laughing lips are singing "Trancadillo,"
With dream of starry skies and ocean billow.

The boisterous game has ceased upon the sward,
And down to rest they sink with one accord:
Here, too, the breath of music floats along
Their ranks, and rises into pensive song.

May be, the ballad of a simple maid,
Who left, she knew not how, her cottage shade;
Led on by wiser, gentler folk, who thought
To make a lady, since a baron sought! —

Ah! left the rough and honest throbbing heart
Of her sweet lover, for the smoother part
Of jewelled matron, waited on, — to die
For love and freedom, work and poverty! —

Who snatches up her baby, running fast
Beyond the gateway, till the Hall is passed;
And sobs and sings, and dreams a moment he
Is laughing on her loving peasant's knee.

Or else it is a song of olden time,
When clinking glasses rang out to the rhyme,
And hands in masonry of love did clasp,
Warmed with the cheer that locked old friendship's
    grasp.

The day is closing: must they rise and go?
So things do have their ending here below:
Blessèd the hour that groweth on and on
Deeper and richer, fuller, yet is never gone! —

The hour that wears the freshening dew of youth;
The hour that blossoms in immortal Truth;
Into to-day, to-morrow never wrought;
Unbroken by the joys that are, and then are not!

They move along upon their homeward way
In silence, night and earth's dim melody:
The elders speak, in undertone, of days
Like these, of old, though better, sweeter far, always!

'The young man, sitting near the maid so still,
Is satisfied even now, if so she will
(While he is looking deep into her eyes)
Point out to him the stars and their sweet ministries.

The valley opens now to take them home;
The village slumbers waking till they come;
Fair forms are dallying, — now they creep from sight;
Sweet voices linger on the air: good-night, good-night!

THE GERMAN LESSON.

THEY sat together many a winter's eve,
When blew the winds without, and brightly shone
The fire upon the wall, and flashed its light
On a youth's face; while deep and blacker grew
His eyes with every gleam, and glowed upon
A beauteous maiden's, till they browned away
Unto a gentle softness.   Yet not o'er
One page they sat, like them who read of old
The tale of Launcelot and sweet Ginevra:
Each held a book, being a space apart;
Yet not so far but some magnetic chain
Might run between, had it so pleased them both!
And one was ready, had he dared, to throw
A trembling chord electric from his heart;
But, ah! he feared 'twould find no resting-place,
And come all quivering back.   So there it staid,
And kindled up a fire within his eyes:
I marvel that the maiden saw it not.

They read together o'er the nervous page
Of high-strung Schiller, he who hath set on
Many a youth to seek a nobler fame,
And love and liberty.   The maiden warmed:
Her woman's soul beat high and tenderly
In the great Poet's presence, who was pure
As heart of woman.   She was following him
In full pursuit after the fair Ideal:
She knew not she was leaving there behind
A living, breathing love, nobility,
And truth, to which the fairest Romance and
The loftiest Poesy gleamed cold and chill
As marble lips before the quivering glow
Of Life.   Alas! why are we always up
Among the skies, when Grace doth wreathe itself
Around the poor tents that we've pitched below,
And radiant Love is at the very door,
All ready to stream in, and light it up?

'Tis true, when they came down again, — she and
The Poet, — she did smile upon the youth;
Yet it was only that the maid was pleased
Because they went so high.   But what knew he,
Poor youth! how many leagues they'd flown up in
The realms of Fancy, when he all the time
Saw only her?   What cared he where she went,

So, through the ambient air of Poesy,
She vanished not from sight?

.   . The maid was touched
With a sweet hope to reach the nameless beauty
That haunts the Poet's dreams.   The youth was fired
With a reality: he *saw* it in
Her face and soul.

Yet, when the village clock
Each time struck out the hour when he was used
To close the book, and go, he punctual rose,
Bade her a stiff " Good-night! " and left the room
Like the unlimbered Schoolmaster.   Not more
Rebellious was the urchin at his task,
Who chafed and fretted in his seat to see
The open sky, than his unruly heart,
That beat about, and strove to press him back
Again to the sweet air of Love.

Yet he
Knew how to rule; but this was sterner stuff
Than he had grappled with, — this rebel heart,
All fortified with mightiest power of Earth.
Yes, Love, thou couldst subdue the Schoolmaster,
And do whate'er thou wouldst with him.   Ah! could

The boys have seen him as he homeward went,
How thou didst pull him back at every step,
They would have joined their hands in thine, and
    said
Thou wert the very likeliest rogue of all.

So every week he through the dark night went
All warm and gay and eager, and came forth,
From out the lightsome room, chilled through, and
    crushed
And maddened by his own unbroken silence.
He seemed to see himself uprising there
An everlasting glacier unto her,
His Sun; and, though the intensity of heat
Was wearing him away *within*, untouched
Without, before the summer of her look,
He stood there cold, serene, unchangeable:
Far better had she, with a scorching hate,
Dissolved him from her presence evermore.

At length the last night came; and he rose up,
Bade her farewell, and gave to her one look
Of love unutterable — (in that look,
All his long tenderness and agony
Leaped from its pent-up silence, and spoke through
Those eyes); — and went out from her face for ever.

She saw it now! and, when his echoing steps
Died fast away, she started up, and then
She sank her head, and mused in a strange sadness.
Ah! had she *loved*, she would not have sat there:
She would have flung herself upon the night,   ·
And called him back with such a love-rent voice,
That he had shortly been upon her breast.
No, no, poor lover! not there canst thou rest
Thy head.   Go thou, and still thy fevered heart
Upon the bosom of the world: 'tis rough
Indeed; but trust her; she knows well thy ails;
For she hath curèd many a heart like thine,
Or bound it up, so that it drifted through
This troublous sea, and reached the shore at last.

THE FORESHADOWING OF SPRING.

BENEATH the languid sky my Spirit loves to lie,
  And bathe herself all o'er in witching sadness:
Her wings she doth unfold, the heavens are fair out
    rolled,
  And now she floats away in idle gladness.

I love the South wind breathing, as, round old Winter
    wreathing,
  She melts his spirit with her gentle sighing;
As tender-nursèd flowers craze us for Summer bowers,
  While yet the snow in woodland nooks is lying.

I love the gentle haze that dulls the glittering blaze
  Of pallid wintry sun, that warmeth not:
It melts my charmèd heart; and, when the fountains
    start,
  She weepeth tears of sweet, poetic thought.

I love the sunlight playing, and longer, longer staying
  Upon my wall each Spring-tide afternoon:
It waketh mystic longing, — fair visions on me throng-
    ing
  Of silver-voicèd May and golden June.

Ah, Soul! they're never granting the joys for which
    thou'rt panting, —
  Not May's young buds, nor June with all her roses!
Not *here* thou'lt find thy Spring nor peaceful Summer-
    ing:
  'Tis *there* thy hope in full delight reposes!

Art weary, then, of striving, and never yet arriving?
  Mightier the boon when it is grasped by thee!
Go on with thy sweet dreaming amidst a world of
    seeming:
  Diviner will at last the waking be!

THE BROKEN HOME.

THEY bore her all the night with faces pale,
Nearer and nearer to the sleeping vale,
    Where, in sweet blossoming,
    She waved at early Spring, —
Cut down before the Summer grass was withering.

They followed close upon her, — father, mother;
And, slow behind, the sister and the brother:
    They spoke not, soft or loud;
    They saw her in her shroud,
And looked with awe and dread around upon each
    other.

They drew nigh to the lindens by the gate:
The willows, with bowed head, did mutely wait.
    Why stirreth not the house?
    Why do they not arouse?
It was not *always* still when they came home so late!

They do not sleep, — they hear the passing feet
They will not come, they cannot come, to meet!
    But when they ope the door,
    And rest upon the floor,
With dull and heavy fall, the burden which they
    bore,

It jarred the stillness there within, — that sound
Ringing so hollow all the house around!
    Slender and lithe and white,
    As poplar in moonlight,
The little sister came down stairs with frightened
    bound.

She clung upon the brave young man, her brother:
. Before her grief his sobs he could not smother;
    He turned away, and durst
    Not look on her at first,
Nor speak a gentle word, lest they should strong out-
    burst.

When from afar he came in pleased delight,
He used to praise her beauty morn and night:
    Though grown to womanhood,
    A trembling child she stood;
And he alone could calm her wild young pulse's flood.

At length he spoke, and made her dry eyes
  weep;
And told her how *she* sang herself to sleep,
  And how her head she prest
  Upon the mother's breast,
With dreamy, dying words of love for all the rest.

So they together wept and calmed again,
Or fell asleep with sudden-starting pain;
  But, ere the morning light
  Made gray the lingering night,
Down swept the clouds before the day with heavy
  rain.

More dread than midnight soon became the morn;
The lurid lightning paled their faces worn;
  The long, low thunder rolled,
  As if a requiem bold,
For all mortality that was and is, it tolled!

Oh, terrible it is to be with death, —
Alone with stiffened clay, without its breath,
  When Nature glooms the while;
  Ere yet we see the smile
Beyond, where its fair soul in sunlight hovereth!

But, hush ! how sacred, sweet, came forth the day
When they were going to lay the loved away !
    The earth seemed holier ;
    No flower or leaf astir :
All pensive ceased their work in honor unto *her*.

She lies within the cheerful, hallowed room
Where once were always smiles, and never gloom ;
    And wild young spirits roving,
    And gentle fireside loving,
And guests who in and out were ever gayly mov-
    ing.

She need not make it sad ; for she reposes,
All covered o'er with lilies and with roses :
    Only she used to wear
    The lilies in her hair ;
Now she, with claspèd hands, them on her breast
    encloses !

Gently the minister the Gospel read ;
For he was near of kin to the sweet dead :
    Ah ! hers was kinship wide ;
    For who was not allied
In love unto that beauteous girl, the country's pride ?

The young men and the maidens, in a ring,
Stood round her lone piano there, to sing
 The hymn she loved the best, —
 Such hymn as calms the breast,
And speaks of peace in God, and endless, endless
 rest.

Then all arose, and went out at the door:
Her gray horse faithfully — as when, before,
 He drew her, crowned with flowers,
 To all the laughing bowers —
Unto the graveyard went to leave her evermore!

She sleeps, she sleeps: they know that she is gone!
They miss her in the evening and at morn:
 The stranger there who came,
 And heard them speak her name
With words so hushed and sweet, now tones his voice
 the same.

·'Twas not her looks, — though she of womanhood
Was fairest; nor her deeds, — though she was good:
 It was because *she loved*,
 That, wheresoe'er she moved,
Amid the old and young, queen ₐo'er all hearts she
 stood!

She sleeps ; but she shall walk in loveliness
Adown the future years, with fond caress
    From every passer-by
    On her sweet memory,
Winning from mortals fairest immortality !

AN AUTUMN WALK.

WHAT aileth thee, thou art so sad to-night,
O Nature? — say, what is it weighs on thee?
Thou art as calm, and noiseless too, as death.
I cannot even hear thee *sigh* amid
The trees.   If thou wouldst break thy apathy,
Thy endless quietude, I'd talk and weep with thee;
Nor ask one single, golden smile upon
The river waiting here so patiently.
And yet thou'rt sweet, like a poor, love-crushed girl,
Who careth not that she is beautiful;
And, all unmindful of the hand of friend,
Or of the voice of childhood, still bespeaks
A gentle, uninvited sympathy.

I rustle 'mong the leaves to rouse thee up.
Not that! — it minds thee how thou didst deck out
The dying Summer, ere she did depart;
Who gave a sickly smile at her new. dress,
With flush upon her cheek, and sank away.

I will betake me homeward; for I see
There is no high commúne with thee to-night:
But, when the gray Morn comes to meet thee, thou
Perchance wilt burst into a shower of tears!

QUILTING AND HUSKING.

I.

THE QUILTING.

HIGH up among the attic beams
There is a great old airy room:
The golden sun in silence streams
Adown the roof, and cheers the gloom.
'Tis lonely through the summer day;
'Tis dreary at the winter night: '.
It hears afar the children play,
But never sees their wild delight.
And yet a pleasant look and kind
It hath, like some old-fashioned face,
That calleth troublous days to mind,
And wears a thousand memories.

The ancient clock all hushed appears,
And keenly stareth out the hours:
The very Time he served for years
Has paralyzed his vital powers.

The spinning-wheel is foundered on
A crumbling shelf of brick and clay;
The wheel the sun doth gleam upon;
The shuttle fades in dark away.
A pillion hangeth good as new;
A gilded coat that figured grand
At country muster, to review
The young militia of the land;
And books with covers stiff and hard
As old theology therein;
Or scattered leaves of gentle bard,
Who talks of love, and not of sin;
Or sorry pages of Romance,
Blurred with the tears of stolen glance.

The mice are pattering at their will
Along the ledges, peeping down
To watch the melons on the sill,
Lest they perchance too ripe have grown;
While luscious odors go and come,
Blent with the scent of herbs that dry
Upon the floor, — sweet marjoram
And pleasant summer savory.

But we are prosing on our way:
The old room is not still to-day!

Behold the Quilt that opens wide
With joints that hoarsely creak, and sway
It rickety from side to side!

The bustling housewife sitteth still
Awhile from all her thousand cares,
Driving her needle with the will
That sent the broom along the stairs.

And thin and sour maidenhood
Is here with her forebodings ill,
To drop them round in bitter mood, —
A wholesome and religious pill.

And gentle single lady, — best
And sweetest being God has made;
Whom He hath left the loneliest
To blossom pale within the shade,
While all around with fruit are blest:
That she afar such fragrance sweet
May send, the young unto her feet
Shall come to feel her sanctity,
And learn of her to live and die.

The village gossip prateth free
And fearlessly of things that *are*,
Or (what is better, sweeter far)
So cautiously of what *may be*.

And romping maidens sit and sew,
With little smothered jests that half
From nothing come, to nothing go,
So easy 'tis for girls to laugh!

Yet it is hard for Meggie: see!
The one who works so pensively,
The maiden with the deep-gray eyes,
Who very quietly doth sew,
Yet draws her breathing hard, as though
She shut beneath a world of sighs.
She thinks how Richard bowed to-day
As they two met upon the way;
How quick he turned his looks in haste
Aside, as though he said a fair
" Good-morning " unto her, and there
It ended, — more he could not waste!
She hears the hum of talk go round;
Upon her ear as far-off speech
It comes, a drowsy, murmuring sound, —
But not a word her soul doth reach;
Click go the needles in and out.
" Say, Meggie, what dost think about? "
Said buxom Nell, who near her sat:
" Thou draw'st thy needle in without
The thread, and what's the use of that? "

She starteth up with sudden flush
Of fear, that spreadeth more and more,
And runneth down with purple blush
Upon her neck so white before ;
And some confusèd words doth say,
" Her head is aching dull to-day : "
Yet back she fell into the maze
Of tangled thoughts that set ablaze
Her heart with little fears that grew
To certainty within her view.
The old room spun around her head ;
Yet on she worked with nervous dread.

And now at length the young men meet
To join them in their simple treat ;
But Meggie lifteth not her eye
Till Richard ere long passes by,
And calls " Good-even " cheerfully,
As he were not ashamed to say
It boldly, and go on his way.

The girls from out their seats do run,
Impatient for the sport and fun ;
But Meggie's stint is never done.
She sews, and passes now a joke —
A poor and pallid thing — to choke

The fluttering in her bosom, lest
The old ones see her throbbing breast.

And Richard whiles the moments well :
He laughs and talks with buxom Nell,
And all the time in Meggie's view !
She's not afraid of Nell, 'tis true,
Who giggles loud, and romps so too ;
But little, sweet-mouthed, laughing Fan,
He likes to be with her, 'tis plain :
The smiles are always on her cheeks,
Though very few the words she speaks.
She's watching, wheresoe'er she goes,
Her old grandmother ; smooths her clothes,
And threads her needle ; finds her case,
With never spectacles therein,
And looks for them in every place,
Nor tires of putting them within.
Ah ! Richard — how can he but see
How dutiful and sweet is she ?
Poor Meggie ! keep the tear-drops back !
The gossip — she will see, alack !
And count them o'er, and they will grow
So many that she cannot keep
Them.   Ere to-morrow night, she'll show
How 'tis for love that Meg doth weep.

And on she stitched; she worked away;
The little diamonds in she stitched;
So fast from out her fingers they
Do grow, they think she is bewitched.
The old ones say she quilts the best
Of all, and is the handsomest.
The centre is a golden star,
Made up of rays from near and far;
It shineth into Meggie's face;
Before her eyes it seems to run,
The colors blending all in one.
A stitch or more within its place, —
And then, behold! the Quilt is done;
A stitch or more from Meggie's hand!
Her dizzy brain is turning fast:
The idle gazers round do stand.
" The Quilt is done!" they cry; "and she
Who chanced to put a stitch the last,
The very first shall wedded be!"

Sweet Meggie starts in quick surprise:
She seems to see the star arise,
And gaze on her with tender eyes,
Then slowly sink before her sight:
So sinks her star of love and light,
And youth and joy, in deepest night!

II.

THE HUSKING.

They sit amid the silken corn:
It is a sweet October morn;
The sky is warm and mellow 'neath
The calm, benignant Autumn sun;
And not a whisper or a breath
Of luscious, balmy air doth run
Throughout the leaves to break the peace
Of Nature's golden harvest ease.

Sweet Meggie's head is very fair,
And softer than the silken ear:
A deeper gold is in her hair
Than gleams from out the husks anear;
But, ah! it fades, — the ripening grace
Of russet youth, that took the place
Of paleness once upon her face.

A pretty sight it is to see
How all are working busily;
And, when the baskets hold no more,
The sunburnt striplings heave their weight
Outrolled upon the granary floor,
And come and go with shining freight.

What pleasant rustling all around,
That mingles with a murmuring sound!
Like summer brook that hummeth on,
Or laugheth out in sport anon,
The tide of talk is rippling low;
Then onward, wilder, it doth go,
And breaketh into noisy flow:
And now it ebbs again; and they,
Industrious, rip the husks away.
The air is still, except within
The barn the cricket chirpeth in
The new-mown hay; and so he sings,
And deeper silence on them brings.

But what is this? The Red Ear! see!
And Meggie findeth it: 'tis she!
Oh! what a boisterous, sudden shout
From all the youths and maids comes out!
Up jump they quick in wild delight,
And tip the baskets in their fun.
A forfeit! Draw the lots aright,
And see who 'tis shall kiss her! Run!
She blushes deep all o'er her face,
And creeps into a quiet spot.
Look, look! 'tis Richard draws the lot!
He runs into her hiding-place.

She trembles in a lovely fright;
And, as her cheek he kisses bold,
Her mouth is smiling so in spite
Of her sweet modest self, behold!
He kisses her upon her lips;
And quick among the crowd he dips,
To 'scape the showering jokes that fly
From out the noisy company.

And now the frolic is begun:
Sweet Meggie dares not lift her eye;
For Richard he is always by.
He helps her when she tears her gown,
And drives the ugly nail adown;
He catches her at Fox and Geese;
And, in the dance, she ever sees
Him opposite, or trembling feels
Him watch to take her down the reels.

The hours of day are fading fast;
The huskers now are turning home:
Her sweet excitement cannot last;
The flush upon her cheek is past,
And pale uncertainty is come.
They leave the threshold one by one,
And Meggie lingers there alone.

She picks the Red Ear from the floor,
And stands, and looks it o'er and o'er.
But, hark! a rustling she doth hear.
She turns: 'tis Richard standing near.
She drops the corn with arm that shook;
He with a sober face doth stand:
" Fair Meggie, does it burn thy hand?
Wast thou ashamed to have me look?
The Red Ear, was it so to blame, —
The little Red Ear, — that it came
To know how I have longed to kiss
Thee, Meggie, and permitted this?"

Her tears are dropping on the ground;
But not a word she hath to say:
Her head she will not turn around.
" I love thee: go thou not away
Till thou hast heard."   She lifts her eyes, —
" Thou lovest me since *yesterday*," —
And looks at him in calm surprise.

" O Meggie! did I give thee pain?
And so I would again, again,
Could I those little tears behold.
The young men said that thou wast cold;

Thou caredst not a single straw
For all the gallants, young or old:
Thy love 'twas folly waiting for."

" And so for *them* I do not care ! "
She says.   He looks her in the face, —
The sweet confession rising there, —
And draws her quick to his embrace,
And kisses off the tears that rise,
And change to smiles within her eyes:
" Dear love! I was but trying thee."
" Ah! never, never jest," said she.
" Dost think 'twas easy, then, for me?
Did I not know that thou wast fair,
With all the rest beyond compare, —
The sweetest maiden quilting there?
And saw I not how swift did fly
Thy little fingers silently? —
None but the old ones staying by;
And I of envy like to die,
That they could sit so near to thee!
I thought, ' If she would only drop
One little look, this game I'd stop.'
Ah, Meggie! thou wast proud, — wast proud ! "
She gently smiled, and shook her head:
Her face upon his neck he bowed.

" I did not love thee less," he said,
For that, thou little haughty maid."

So on his arm sweet Meggie leant;
And forth, at set of sun, they went
Along the meadow where the brook
Was wandering in a willowy nook,
And sang the lonely Whippoorwill
Awhile, till all the night was still:
Then rose the Hunter's Moon to light
Them home to sweetly dreaming night.

THE NORTHERN LIGHTS.

Lo! in the chambers of the North
A wondrous brightness streameth forth!
Are those cold lands afraid of night,
Impatient for the warm sunlight?
Can they not for Aurora wait,
But must that wondrous light create?

Yes, strangely beautiful are ye,
Nor ever chill or cold to me;
Those truly are not melting beams,
But strong, inspiring radiant gleams.
Yon Polar climes in earth or sky
Speak words with meaning great and high.
The Southern gales may gently fan
The feeble breast of fainting man;
But, oh! drink in, ye firm and strong!
That living breath, and ponder long
Upon those stars so clear and bright,
And on that mystic wall of light,

Till in yourselves at length may be
Some spark in which perchance ye'll see
The grand old North's immensity.

Remember him, that glowing heart,
Who dared to make himself a part
Of strong defiant Nature there ;
And, 'mid the breath of Polar air,
Did win her unto friendship by
The earnest reverence of his eye,
And showed her to the gaze of men,
And died — to live immortal then.

The sons of Norway well might deem
Those glittering spears the dazzling gleam
From lances wielded by the hand
Of heroes in Walhalla's land ;
Or Indian see the red deer bound
From arrows glancing all around
In the Eternal Hunting-Ground.

Nightly Aurora, Northern Light !
Exalt our souls to lofty flight !

WAITING FOR DEATH.

SHE was alone, save one who there did stand —
The strong old nurse — all day with decent hand
To smooth the pillow or to give the cup, —
The cordial which must hold her being up,
Though she in death would gladly let it drop.

The early raptures of foretasted heaven,
When she herself to Death had willing given,
Were fading; for he tarried long and late:
Her wings, once fluttering to the upper gate,
At length hang heavy, — for 'tis hard to wait.

" Farewell, good Life!" she said exultingly:
" Thou hast been kind; but they are calling me!
I leave the robes, which thou hast given, with thee;
And through the night haste, ere those voices fly!" —
But down she fell, upon the verge of it,
So weary; and Death would not take her yet!

She heard the bell that told how cold did lie
The little child, of late so warm his breast,
With springing heart, quick gathered to his rest;
While she, unclothing of mortality,
Was yet not as the fair immortals drest:
Not claimed of Life or Death, — midway between, —
She lived not with the unseen or the seen!

The Summer passed with balmy breath by her:
She felt it warm her cheek, and heard it stir
The curtains of her still and dusky room.
But, ah! in rosy bloom she saw it not;
And yet she lay not there inwrapt in gloom:
"I shall go hence with it," she fondly thought.

The Autumn winds sang over Summer's bier,
And strewed the dry leaves for a winding-sheet;
But she, though faded too, must linger here:
No dirge for her lost bloom was sounding yet.

The Winter gathered darkly in the sky;
The snow-clouds thickened in the air around;
And lighter than the early flakes that lie
In trembling haste, and melt upon the ground,
Upon the lap of life she fluttering lay,
Waiting in vain to be dissolved away.

Yet scorned she not the earth, nor did despise
Our little mortal doings here below:
She marked the blue of heaven, — the glittering snow;
She hoped the bells rung merry to and fro;
And asked the maiden, with faint smiling eyes,
How fared it with her lover, and if he
Would come at Christmas, — or before, maybe.
For childlike Patience on her sat, more sweet
Than e'en the high delight which once she wore,
When she was borne in ardent thought before
Unto the immortal life with eager feet.

Ah! many a one there is who sweetly dies
In some strong hour of mighty sacrifice;
Or in the grasp of swift-descending fate,
When terrors piled on terrors threatening wait;
Or in the eternal calm that falleth deep,
When maddening fever ends its whirlwind sweep!

But she must feel for weeks and months his breath,
And look for him at eve or morning light;
And lie, throughout the endless shadowy night,
With senses all undimmed and vision bright,
Figuring the ghastly semblances of death;
And meet the morrow, to replume anew
Her spirit for the last great journey through.

There is release, — there is release for all;
For when the Spring stole forth again, to call
With gentle sighs the world from out its grave,
It came — that hour — like half the things we crave,
Yet dread, — came lightly when she knew it not:
That hour, for which her fainting soul had sought
All of its scattered energies to save,
Came like some flitting morning dream at last;
And so she to her Maker's bosom passed.

SIMPLICITY.

TO THE NEW-ENGLAND MAIDEN.

KNOW thou, O Lady! there is nought that sits
On thee more comely than Simplicity:
The Poet ever flingeth it o'er thee;
And wilt thou cast it off, and say it fits
Alone the rustic maid, who queens it in
A robe 'twere well if thou again couldst win?

Hast thou known distant climes and pageantry?
Remember, thou hast never seen pretence
In Nature's face; and learn not to dispense
(Because thou hast with courts perchance been free)
Aught more refined than simple courtesy,
Nor load thyself with foreign spoils from thence.

Perhaps thou learnèd art in books? — canst speak
Of all philosophies? Bethink thee, then,
How Wisdom sat upon those ancient men,
In a simplicity serene and bare
As beauty on the marble of the Greek,
And bade the dullest one talk with her there.

A genius art thou?   Let thy soul's firelight
Play soft around, and come and go about,
Unconscious as thy breathing, and without
The thought of self; nor with display so bright
Glare thou, that men, all shamed with their own night,
Do fear thy greatness, nor their own find out.

Canst walk in Beauty's airy triumph high, —
Crowds on thy skirts, whom thou dost stop and pay
Now with a smile or two, to keep them by?
Thy noblest slaves will surely drop away,
Dost thou thy fairness school with complex art,
Nor let it speak itself unto the heart.

But hast thou none of these, — only a dear
And lovely spirit which doth grateful meet
The pleased heart of the world, as falleth sweet
Childhood's fond utterance on the mother's ear?
Strongest art thou in Love's simplicity:
Ah! thou shalt win all men to worship thee!

THE SPIRIT OF AUTUMN.

BEHOLD the woodland tops that deck the land!
See them burst forth in glory's ripening blaze!
How close yon brotherhood of trees doth stand,
And put forth all its strength at once to raise
Aloft that hanging of fair tapestries,
With gold and red inwove, unto the skies;
As some old festive towers compactly rise
On airy hillside, and afar are gleaming,
One sheet of many-colored draperies streaming!
The sombre massive Pines stand low in front,
Even as some stern, grim, iron portal, wont
To fright away all entrance at the gate.
But is it dark within with sombre state?
No, no! above, those rainbow pennons call
The guest at early morn and evening late.
Is there not joy and highest festival
In this and every radiant queenly hall,
Where enters beauteous Autumn at the doors,
And treads her crimson-leafèd damask floors?

She is not gay: so her they do not meet
With loudly echoing mirth and carolling,
And freaks of laughter, as when sunny Spring
Bounds forth so young and frolicsome and sweet!
But how subdued she steps, with gracious mien,
Even as of olden days some sainted queen,
Who walks adored with calm, majestic feet,
While her deep eyes are full of peace serene!
A golden halo spreads around her face:
She seems to hold communion with the unseen;
And, as she passeth in, she casts a grace
Which doth with sudden glow irradiate
The looks of those who in her presence wait;
And they, ere long, themselves do all subdue
Unto a sweet and high solemnity,
Which melts into a mystic harmony,
That, like the murmuring sea, doth whisper through
The pinewood arches, and in lightness floats
'Mid the red-maple windows, till on high,
Unto the grand mosaic roof, the notes
At length rise up, a mighty symphony!
Hark! hear them sing her praise exultingly,
While she doth kneel, her face unto the sky,
Inwrapt in dreams of immortality: —

Glorious Lady! sweeter far
Than the Spring's young glances are,
Or her winning coquetries,
Is the light within thine eyes.

Heavenlier than the ripening grace
Of the ardent Summer's face
Is the smile which, like a dream,
Ever round thy lips doth gleam.

Richer than May's flaxen hair,
Waving sportive on the air,
Is thy auburn brown so meek,
Resting on thy brow and cheek.

Lovelier than the flush of rose
O'er young June that comes and goes
Are the deeper blooms that glance
Over all thy countenance.

Thou art holiest of the three;
They are children unto thee:
Thou hast dreams which they know not;
Thou art touched with highest thought.

But, O beauteous saint! to be
In thy rapturous moods with thee!
Who could turn him from that hour,
Stirred not by thy wondrous power?

When, before the silent sky,
Thou in golden trance dost lie,
In thy peace beatified,
Who could tear him from thy side?

Let thy sisters, then, be gay,
Happy spirits in their way:
Thou hast found the better part,
Autumn, for thou *blessèd* art.

S U N D A Y.

———

Sweet day! shall I dare speak of thee,
When holy Herbert sings so well,
And far along the past I see
A line of saintly souls, who tell
Thy graces, breathing from their lyres
High, aromatic, pious fires?

White-winged thou sitt'st as cherub in
Thy peaceful seat above the week,
To brood in freshness o'er the din
Of daily heat, with pleadings meek;
And to the good man's fading eye
Thou light'st the track of memory.

Thy vanished treasures at his touch
Shed fragrant odors on his soul;
And, should his spirit faint o'ermuch,
The sacred Past shall make him whole,
And drop on his discouragement
As healing balm by angels sent.

What stillness on the Country falls!
She folds her hands, and sayeth grace;
And e'en the City smooths its walls,
And frames its worldly battered face
To piety, and so doth pray
And sing the holy hours away.

Day of the Lord! — when first he broke
In beauteous majesty on men,
And to the weeping Mary spoke,
And glorified the earth again! —
Shine on our land, that she may rest
From sin and labor on his breast.

Come, risen Master! shine that we
May see the truth that dwells above!
Lift all thy churches unto thee,
And fold them on thy heart of love!
Come, sanctify them ever by
The holy bonds of charity!

Beloved New England's old and young
Go forth when morning bells do chime:
There is no sound of noisy tongue,
No masquerade of foreign clime.
Lord Jesus! pray with her that she
May worship God in truth like thee!

"THE SILENT WAY."

———

IT is a little opening sweet
That leads throughout the wood, and stills
The weary heart: a presence fills
This rare and wonderful retreat,
Which all the very being thrills.

Think not 'tis named because a gloom
Is brooding o'er it, like a bird
Of night within the forest heard:
'Tis rather like a sacred room,
Amid the noise of day unstirred.

The winds of March come sweeping by;
But, ah! they cannot enter there:
The burning sun of August air
Peeps through the leaves, and longs to lie
And cool him, — but he may not dare.

The frosts of pale November chill
The heart of earth: but there they fling
Around a crimson carpeting;
And, last, a mantle white, that will
Be never scanty there till Spring.

But go at sweet Midsummer night:
The pines with showers are spicy yet;
The birches tremble at the set
Of sun, in pale transfigured light;
And low the savin clusters wet.

Go on between the tangled walls
Of shining twigs, that drop the rain;
Then round the hill, to greet again
The purple day before it falls,
And breathe the clover on the plain.

THE OLD FARMHOUSE.

———

IT stands within the hollow by the road:
See you not how the plenteous barn doth show
Its turret, nestling warm in that abode,
Secure from all the gusty winds that blow?

We seem to reach it; yet we are not there,
The path runs in and out so waywardly.
But we shall tire not; for the boundless air
Sweeps on our cheeks from off the azure sea.

The blithesome Apple-trees keep company
Along the mossy wall, and beckon on
With kindly looks that touch the passer-by
With thoughts of rustic ease and harvests won;

And mellow cheer within the farmer's gate;
And lover in the kitchen, winter's night;
And schoolboy — full his pocket — running late,
With stuffed-out cheek, like squirrel in a fright.

Now come we to the lane : each side, abreast,
They stand, with honest yeoman courtesy ;
And up we pass, until at length we rest
Content beneath the great old Willow-tree, —

The Willow-tree that fronts the barn in pride,
And rocks the simple farm-yard bird to sleep,
And feels the gray cat scrambling up its side,
Chasing her kitten, while the moonbeams creep.

The Lilac clusters soft about the door,
And swells her buds at dream of far-off Spring,
To melt away in purple bloom, before
The breath of June her scent of rose doth fling.

The Oriole hangs his jaunty nest on high,
And starts the modest Bluebird on her way,
Till gold and blue are meeting in the sky,
And ripple fast his notes with her smooth lay.

The Ox quiescent in his manger looks,
And ponders on the nothingness of man :
" All flesh is grass."   The God of Brahmin books
Shall find him wise disciple in his van.

9

Around, the Cows are cropping at their ease
The spicy hay that showers adown the space,
O'erhung with spiders' wreaths, that floating tease
The farmer's eyes from every darksome place.

Though, here and there, an eager mother stands
With neck erect, and wandering, frenzied eye,
Calling her little one, who in the hands
Of stranger rude went out at morn to die.

But when at eve the mellow sunlight streams
Above the door, and climbs up slowly, where
It plays in streaks of gold among the beams,
One deep, soft rustle rises on the air —

From out the faithful herd, who trustfully
Await their daily bread in peace from Heaven;
From Him who watcheth with a tender eye
The little sparrow in his nest at even.

No minster ever wore a sweeter calm;
No purer incense rose than their warm breath;
No worshippers, unfearing every harm,
Obey so well the God of Life and Death.

And here the tenants pass their peaceful days
Within the raftered parlor long and low,
And fain would fashion to it all their ways,
And in the healthful olden spirit grow.

So, should the comely housewife, stepping light,
Or ancient goodman, from their shades appear,
They may not turn away ashamed at sight
Of such unwonted quiet dwellers here.

MISCELLANEOUS POEMS.

THE WEDDING PRESENTS.

GOOD Charlemagne was dead. The solemn chant
Was lingering yet amid the stillness of
The chapel aisles within the royal walls
Of ancient Thermes, whence of late they bore
Him to his resting-place, and left him there, —
The glorious monarch, — dead and cold e'en as
The meanest fighter in his myriad ranks;
And colder, mayhap, — since the vaults of Aix
Relaxed them never to the warming sun,
That gazed all day in friendliness upon
The soldier's trampled grave of grass and stones!

And Louis sat upon his father's throne,
Presumptuous, as though he'd ruled the land
For threescore years; nor troubled he his head
Once to bethink him how it chanced that death
Took hence that grand old man, — else were *he* but
A mean, disloyal subject still, and son!

They called him, too, the Debonnaire, forsooth!
Men knew not why; for he was cold and hard
And sullen as old Thermes' frowning walls,
Save when he broke a keen and bitter jest,
That chilly ran throughout his courtiers' veins,
And froze their smiles to pale obsequiousness.

Sweet Gisla and Rotrude lived there within
The castle-gates, — the old King's daughters fair;
And emperors had sought to win their hands:
But Charlemagne would have them mind their hearts,
Nor sternly bade their hands go opposite;
Nor forced the gentle girls to wed, as kings
And queens are wont to do, with made-up smiles
Of courtly resignation on their brows.
And so these emperors bowed themselves away,
Much wondering at the curious maids, who seemed
So weary when they talked of all their lands
And pleasure-palaces, that were like heaven
Compared unto these gloomy castle walls.
Somehow they could not light them up, these fair
Young sisters, unto talk and gayety;
And yet men said they were the stars that burned
In roundelays, and gleamed athwart the sword
Of many a frenzied knight, and twinkled round
The brave and merry Tournament of France.

They felt there was a hidden smile, in truth,
Beneath the changing rose upon the cheek
Of hushed Rotrude; and that a quiet fire
Was slumbering in young Gisla's blacker eyes,
That well might warm the paleness of her face.
But, ah! they could not wake it up, these poor
Gay puppets in their lace and gold, who learned
Their story, ere they came away from home,
Of councillors and tutors.   So they went;
And chance may be the royal girls did laugh
At all the bungling Teutons' courtesies, —
They born among the flower of chivalry.

The maids *did* love two plainer gentlemen,
With nothing but good swords to call their own,
And swinging forms, and eyes that dared the world,
And big hearts throbbing in their manly breasts,
And hands that played with ladies' locks as light
As they did boldly curb the restless steed.

But Louis, this dear brother, knew how maids
Would throw their beauteousness away, and did
Bethink him brotherly how best to right
This sad mistake.   He frowned not on them; no!
But, musing in a quiet, kingly way,
He said the palace of his sisters was

Not still enough, and he would make it seem
As calm as any cloister, so there should
Be nothing to disturb them.　And he smiled ;
And smiled the sisters too, they knew not why,
Except they wished to please this strange good brother,
Even though his pleasure felt so very like
A shiver as it crept anear their hearts.

Two goodly knights, one eve, ride gayly up
Unto the palace-gates: the seneschal
Receives them with a grim civility
Within the large and silent court.　But, mark !
He bars the gates behind them with a clang ;
And forthwith steps a second officer,
And curtly bids them give to him their swords.
They stand with looks amazed: "What mean ye, men ?
We come as messengers from our good King !"

"Ay, even so, Sir Knights?　How fares he then ?
Long life to him, Louis le Debonnaire !"

"He fares as well as any royal son
Who has been smelling 'mong the tombs these six
Weeks gone, and heard the chanting monks amid
The dampness, till they left the old King there
In peace.　And Heaven have mercy on him now !

But look! take you this letter.   Pray you, read,
Nor be so careful in your dignities;
Seeing 'tis but your *King* — no more, good sirs —
Who bids you ope his castle-doors, and have
A little comfort for two gentlemen
Who're cold and hungry.   Read, nor wait all night:
Yon cursèd flambeau flickers in the court,
And blurs the pages with a muddy light.
A decent keeper does not stay to read
A king's certificate, nor timorous keep
The bearers standing in the courteous wind.
Ho, now! why do you look so blank, and stare
On us as Christian on the Infidel?
No more of all your pretty ceremony!
We'll tell his Majesty, you're not a whit
Behindhand in the rules of etiquette."

He coughed a dry and cheerless cough, — the grim
Old seneschal, — and led the way into
A room with lofty arches, grand enough
To suit the aiming of the proudest knight,
Save that these riders dreamed of chimney-side,
And forms, perchance, that moved in firelight sweet;
Not ancient, sculptured walls and solitude.
Once more he raised the paper to the flame,
And ran his old eyes o'er the kingly page,

As reading to himself: " Raoul de Lys
And Robert de Quercy."

                    " Those are our names.
We come announcing that the King will follow :
Make haste, that we receive him not with thin
And hungry looks and jaded courtesies."

" Sir Knights, you are my prisoners !   Mark you,
It is the King's command, writ on this page !
More, you must be apart : such is his word."

" 'Tis plain as day," said Count de Quercy.   " Look ! "
" In faith," said Raoul de Lys, " '*tis* written here."
" Yes, there is no gainsaying it," said Quercy.
" Nor understanding royal whims," quoth Raoul.

" Haste, gentlemen ; 'tis late.   Come you, De Quercy ;
And stay you here, Baron de Lys."

                    " Well, then,
Good-night ! " said gay De Lys.   " Be cheery, friend :
Ill luck comes not within these walls, that hold
My golden Butterfly with silken touch,
That floats around the dark to light it up !
And there's a dark-eyed Nightingale, that sits,

And sings alone unto her faithful heart :
You'll make her fill this forest of grim walls
With sweetest music on the morrow, knight ! "

The door swung close ; and Raoul sat alone
Upon a step of stone, and pondered long.
" Heyday ! " he said at length.   " Fie, fie ! art thou
A sick old woman, hearing sounds, who shakes
At panelled doors, and ever thinks to run
Away from Death ?   That is the road to him !
Good knight doth never keep so far away
From his dry bones as when he doth forget
The very sound of his old rattling sides,
And sleeps as free as though this Death were not ! "

And so he slept, and dreamed he caught — ah ! sweet —
The Butterfly within his longing hand !
She quivered softly, and was loath to go ;
When, lo ! the Dragon-fly did prick his heart,
And down she fluttered, leaving but the dust
From off her wings to soothe the mortal pains !

He woke, then fell to troublous sleep again.
But hark ! — he starts from sleep !   " Speak ! — who
    is there ? "
He stares with blurrèd eyes upon a light

That breaks upon his dark and silent room.
He shakes the haziness away, and sees
A panel opening in the wall, — so gray,
So strong, and so relentless, when he slept.
'Tis Gisla standing there, so fair and pale ;
Her rich hair thrust beneath a golden comb ;
Her beauteous throat half screened from midnight damp
With silken scarf, that hung adown her arm
And swept the floor, unheeded in her chill
And trembling haste.   She draws De Quercy by
The hand, and gazes in such frighted love
Upon him with her lustrous eyes, he goes
In deep amazement whither way she leads.

He leaped unto his feet, De Lys.   Ah ! now
He was awake, and forward rushed !   " But where
Is she ? — where is Rotrude ? " — " Hush, hush ! she
      comes ! "
And Gisla spoke in whispers.   " Death is near !
Yes, Death is waiting for you, Count de Lys !
And him, — for Robert !   O my Jesu ! quick !
He means to see you lying cold and still !
He hates you, knights !   You were his father's friends !
You love his daughters !   Sainted soul ! he left
Them all alone, with none to care for them, —
His orphan children, — save the two they love.

Save me! O Robert! 'tis a cruel life!
No: save thyself, I pray! Go, go, with Raoul!
Go hence, while I can see thine eye is bright,
And looks on me, and knows me yet thy Gisla!
For he will take thee if thou goest not;
And they will carry thee away, so still,
With not a word of anger from thy lips.
Thou wilt not raise thy hand, or mind the road
That leads where all is cold; nor trouble thee
About the sisters in the castle left.
Thou wilt be dead, De Quercy! hear'st thou not?"

"Calm thee, dear Gisla! See! I kiss thy hand;
And I *will not be dead!* Thou'lt see me live
To dare thy villain brother; ay, just Heaven!"

"Cursed be the prince who plays so foul with us,
His royal father's friends!" said Count de Lys.

"We were his favored pages," said De Quercy.

"Ah, yes!" spoke Gisla softer through her tears;
"And many a night you told us how you watched
The stars with him, till morning came upon
The castle turrets, where he loved to be
With none but you and his high thoughts, and Heaven."

" He dare not do the deed! for Charlemagne
Is scarcely gone from out his seat of glory,
Or wonted to the grave's dead company;
And Louis hath not got a hold upon
The sceptre yet" ——

                " He holds it tight enough
To punish coward subjects! ha!"   And there
He stood — the King! — upon the silent steps
That ran back into darkness, dragging forth
To light the fluttering and fair Rotrude,
Surprised and spent with his unbending grasp:
Her soft locks shook around the brother's arm,
And swam her deep-blue eyes in tears of strange
Amazement, as she looked into his face.
Four solemn guards stood silently behind,   ·
Hooded, and waiting for the King's command.

" Nay, sit you down, Rotrude, my little dove!
Of what are you afraid?   Is't not your brother?
So — nestle down upon this seat of stone:
We're not a hawk to scare the pretty birds.
Come, hear you what we have to say: we know
The way about here in the dark, yet came
We not through all these winding stairways but
To frighten our dear sisters.   Look you here!

These gentlemen will lay aside their hoods,
And help us to a little ceremony."

" A ceremony ? " quoth the knights at once.

" Ay! surely as the nails did pierce Him on
The cross, our reign we will inaugurate —
Ha! — with a double wedding.   Gisla, you
Shall marry Robert, Count de Quercy.   You,
Rotrude, — will you not take Raoul de Lys?
You might have looked a trifle higher ; but
We will not quarrel with a lady's choice :
And then these knights were loved of him, our Sire.
Here are our wedding presents to your lords !"

And forth the guards presented to their gaze
Two costly suits of armor finely wrought.
They blushed, the knights, and thanked their gracious
        King,
And eyed the pieces from afar, abashed,
And stammered broken words of loyalty.

" We have but little faith in human thanks,"
Said Louis ; " and we shall not look for much.
Go you, good sisters ! wear what pleases you ;
Stay not to look on men-at-arms, while they

Are at their toilet, like the peasant girls
Who stare upon the pikemen, curious
To watch while they equip their boorish selves. —
Now, gentlemen! will you put on your suits?"

The four attendants brought the pieces near.
The knights surveyed them with delighted eyes;
Yet cautious moved, irresolute, and smiled
With courteous grace; and lingering, half in doubt,
Half in admiring joy, they stood awhile,
As in a maze of sweet uncertainty.
The King grew restless. " Come, Sir Knights! you
          are
Not so impatient for your brides as we."
So, then, the guards put on the thick brassards,
That fitted wondrous well upon the knights;
And helmets, with the visor closed to light.
Ere long they were equipped, and more, in faith,
For battle than for wedding festival!

The four still men then led them to their seats,
And touched a spring that shut with chilling sound:
The bridegrooms with a nervous tremor start;
Then presently their heads sink drooping down
Upon their breasts, as though they mused of love,
And festive halls, and merry wedding bells.

The belfry of St. Jacques rang out the hour;
And in they came, — the lovely, blushing brides!
The King turned round, and looked upon the knights,
And smiled, and pointed to them, sitting on
Their oaken chairs; and so went gently out.

And foremost was Rotrude: among her curls,
So fair and light, a cord of blue and gold
Lay hid, and wound above her starry eyes;
While on the cold and dusty floor she trailed
The foldings of her silken azure gown.
And Gisla lingered slow behind, with robe
Of richest crimson, unadorned; and but
A gem, which Robert gave her, in her hair.
The lovers sprang not up to meet the brides;
But there they sat, and spoke they not a word.

" Ah, Raoul! wouldst thou make me think thou art
Not glad?   Thou canst not cheat thy Rotrude so!
Through all thy heavy armor, I can tell
How thou art smiling underneath. — The saints!
How cold and stiff it is!   Thou canst not move:
Thou look'st as if thou wert arrayed for fight,
And not to kiss Rotrude. — Come, speak! or I
Shall weep! — Thou didst not use to tease me so!

See! I am crying now like foolish girl:
Thou canst not feel the tears through all this steel."

Then Gisla came anear with wondering eyes:
" God!— Robert! Robert!   He is dead, — is dead!
O Jesu! — Tear it off!   He cannot breathe."

And Gisla threw her arms, in frenzied strength,
About his metal form, and wrenched the springs,
And cold and pale and all unconscious fell
Within her noble lover's warm, dead arms!

Ay! they *were* all equipped for hardest fight!
Alone, beneath the armor's night, that shut
So thick around, they fought for blessed air,
One moment, in a desperate agony,
And yielded to the awful conqueror, Death!,

Note. — The author is indebted for the facts of this poem to
Dr. Doran's " Knights and their Days."
The two suits of armor were sent from Ravenna to Charlemagne.
They were so constructed, that all their openings closed at once by
a spring.

TIME, THE HEALER.

———

BLESSED be Time, that waiteth never, never;
But stealeth, slow and sure, upon its way!
Yes, God be thanked that Now is not Forever; —
That man can look up from his grief, and say,
"*It was;*" when, though his wounds be stiff and sore,
They do not stare upon him, as before,
With open, mocking eyes!   For thou, great Past!
Dost take our pains unto thy bosom vast.

They come apace with rude and blasting breath:
As the fell plague, that brings the thrill of death,
Yet creepeth onward from the house, while men
Pick up their dead, and dare to speak again;
So they to thy deep presence pass, and then
We scan them with a close and steadfast glance,
E'en though, before, one look on them askance
Was terrible, as on they did advance!

Ah, Past! how still, serene, thou art always!
We, too, do grow serener as we gaze,
And stand in statue-like repose the while,
Even as the Virgin Mother in her shrine,
With hands calm folded on her breast benign;
And dream of all the sacredness divine
Around the martyr-heart, till we do smile
Upon our earthly pains, and learn to know
Joy is not best of all things here below!

THE ALPS.

———

THROUGHOUT the early morn we crept along
Amid the genial valleys decked with vines,
And hamlets smiling in their peacefulness,
And hoary towers o'erlooking them above,
With chapel ready, as of old, for prayer.
The song of Troubadour at break of day
Chimed soft and plaintive through our morning dreams;
And Baron's blue-eyed daughters, gleaming out,
Around gray turrets waved their golden hair;
While from dear kindly monks in cloister-walls
Came soft and lulling Aves, intermixt
With distant ring and clash of knightly sword.
We seemèd verily to steal among
The mellow pages of old, fond Romance.

But hush! rouse up, my heart! What saw we then,
As forth we came from out the valley's depth?
The Alps! the Alps! Avaunt, old Past! and take

Thy mouldy relics all along with thee,
And pray and mutter o'er them as thou wilt!
Yes, there they stood together, side by side,
Their foreheads bared to heaven as worshippers,
Perennial freshness resting on their brows;
The glow of youth, the strength of manhood, there;
And there the deep serenity of age.
My heart rang out in high festivity:
I heard them sing a never-ending song, —
"There is no time with God!   His beauty was
And is, and shall be ever, evermore!"

SCHEFFER'S PICTURE OF DANTE AND BEATRICE.

Upon the summit of celestial joy,
Which doth begin and end in peace, she stands,
And reaches out to him her blessed hands.

The peace that groweth with the pains of earth
Was hers; and now the joy of purer rest,
The peace that sinketh deeper in the breast.

She whelmeth all his soul in tenderest awe
And most unutterable reverence:
He gazeth breathless, lest she float from thence.

"O woman! freshening presence! far more sweet
Than the celestial gales to pilgrim given
The flutter of thy garments throughout heaven."

She raiseth up her finger in rebuke:
"Thou must not look for me, but higher light;
Else will the Father veil me from thy sight."

And, oh! she looks so far, so far beyond,
An everlasting vision floating lies
Mirrored within the azure of her eyes.

He bows his head upon his ardent heart;
He calms it with a spirit struggling yet,
And stands subdued before the Infinite.

She watches him with parted lips, and smiles:
He looks; he catches quick the gleams that play
Around her mouth; and, lo! she soars away.

"O Love supreme!" he cries, "thou'rt all in all:
Yet thou hast deigned to robe thyself for me
Within her angel-like humanity.

Then bid this most tumultuous spirit lean
Upon her calmness: so together we
May go up to the heavenly mount and Thee."

CHARLOTTE BRONTÉ.

I SEEM to stand upon Life's very verge;
I've traversed all the experience which it brings:
I am not old; but I have seen all things.
Strange waves have swept my youth with whelming
    surge,
And washed it bare of all illusions sweet, —
Even as the ocean-rock stands bleak and cold ;
Her young green moss, and pebbles all of gold,
And rainbow-shells, swept off by tides that beat.

I will not be like that gray rock at sea!
My rainbow-hopes I'll bring from out the deep,
And lay them where Life's floods can never sweep:
Though now my soul, and not my hair, is gray,
When fades my hair, again my soul shall be
· All young and blooming for Eternal Day !

TO C——.

———

THE book is laid within thy guiding hand;
Do with it what thou wilt, so I may see
Thy smile approving, with a sweet command
To high and nobler labors urging me.

Along the golden heights of Poesy,
Or tender vales of duty and of joy, —
In both my ways, it is thy earnest eye
That points me upward in my loved employ:
Dear Faith and Poesy! may they abide
With us until the night in day is glorified!

THE END.

ل

ERRATA.

Page 59, line 2, for " some pale " read " the great."
Page 77, line 16, for " line " read " lure."

www.ingramcontent.com/pod-product-compliance
Lightning Source LLC
Chambersburg PA
CBHW021109020726
47500CB00003B/667